SO-CFQ-807

Nola The Nurse and Friends

Explore The Holi Fest

She's On The Go Series Vol. 2

by Dr. Scharmaine L. Baker, NP.

illustrated by Marvin Alonso

A DrNurse
Publishing House

A DrNurse Publishing House
New Orleans, Louisiana

Nola The Nurse™ She's On The Go series Vol. 2
Text copyright © 2015 by Scharmaine Lawson-Baker
Illustrations copyright © Scharmaine Lawson-Baker

All rights reserved. No part of this book may be used or reproduced in any manner whatsoever without written permission.
For information address A DrNurse Publishing House
3749 N. Causeway Blvd., Suite B
Metairie, La. 70002
www.NolatheNurse.com

ISBN 978-1-945088-01-8

Library of Congress Control Number: 2016908008

Author Contact info:
info@DrBakerNP.com
@NolaTheNurse
@DrBakerNP
www.DrBakerNP.com
www.NolaTheNurse.com

To Whitney, Skylar, and Wyatt.

Thanks for allowing mommy to be creative and moody.

~Schar

Nola loves playing nurse practitioner and taking care of all her friends' dolls. She also loves wearing the nurse practitioner uniform her mother bought for her.

Her mother is a nurse practitioner with a very busy schedule.

Nola is just seven years old and rides her bike to visit her friends who live nearby.

"Nola, Anita's and Adar's mum called me just now," Mother called out. Nola was in the garden, playing with Gumbo, her very mischievous puppy.

"What is it, Mommy?" Nola rushed in, as she thought most probably her friends' dolls must be sick.

Anita and Adar live in the neighborhood with their family; they are from India. Anita is in a wheelchair. She was in a car accident several years ago, but she still plays on the playground with her friends. They struggle to keep up with her! Anita has a doll named Lady.

Nola's mommy, Eden, explained, "Today all the Indian families are celebrating a festival called *Holi* at the grounds adjoining the hospital."

Nola heard the phone ringing, and she answered. It was her friend Maddi. Maddi has been her friend for two years. Nola loves playing with her because Maddi wants to be a midwife. Midwives are registered nurses who deliver babies. "Are you going to the Holi fest?" Maddi asked.

"Yes, I'm so excited to go!" Nola replied, jumping in the air with excitement.

"Ok. I will meet you there," Maddi said as she hung up the phone and dashed away to prepare for the celebration.

"Since I am going to the hospital now, I can drop you at the grounds," Nola's mother said.

"Mommy, is Anita's doll ok? And how about Adar's doll?" Nola asked. Adar is Anita's brother. Nola has cared for his superhero figure, Clint, in the past.

"Well, in fact all the dolls in the home are sick," Mommy noted. "Come quickly, darling, or Mommy will be late for work."

"Can Bax ride with us, since we have more than one sick doll in the house?" asked Nola.

Meet Bax. Bax's family moved into the house across the street a few months ago. He is eight years old. His family is from China. Bax also loves to play nurse practitioner. When they go to visit a sick doll, he usually rides his skateboard, while Nola rides her bike. Bax also fixes broken bikes, trucks and teddy bears.

Nola told him that he should pick one area that he really likes, because that what nurse practitioners do. They work in special areas. Bax loves superheroes very much, so he wants to be a superhero nurse practitioner.

Nola's mommy said, "Ok, but don't wear the nurse practitioner's uniform today. Anita's mother mentioned that people will be throwing colored water on each other at the Holi festival."

"Ok, Mommy, I will be ready in a minute."

Nola put on a colorful dress, picked up her nurse practitioner kit and was ready to go.

Bax came over, and they all drove to the park.

Mommy dropped Nola and Bax at the playground, and Anita and her family greeted them. Anita had her wheelchair tires painted red in celebration of Holi. Adar was waiting, and he said, "I hope you two can check Clint – he must have the same fever that Anita's doll has."

Nola and Bax reassured Adar, "We're happy to check them all." Everyone knew they were nurse practitioners. Nola and Bax loved to help!

"Yes, both of them are ill. Please help them now," said Anita and Adar. They all rushed away to the sick dolls.

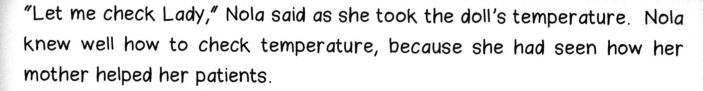

"Let me check Lady," Nola said as she took the doll's temperature. Nola knew well how to check temperature, because she had seen how her mother helped her patients.

"Let me look at Clint," Bax offered. He took Clint's temperature and could tell that he had a fever.

"They are having a fever, and both are very warm," Nola and Bax explained.

"Is it serious?" Anita and Adar asked.

"No, it's just a fever. We will put cool towels on their heads, and they will feel better soon," Nola said.

She opened her nurse practitioner bag and took out a white towel, which she placed on Lady's forehead.

Bax reached into his nurse practitioner bag and placed a cool, fresh towel on Clint's head, as well. "He will feel better real soon," said Bax.

"Now let's join our family at the grounds," suggested Anita and Adar.

"What is the *Holi* festival all about?" Nola and Bax wanted to know.

"Let's ask my mommy; she will give you all the details," said Anita.

"Mum, can you please explain the *Holi* festival to Bax and Nola?" Adar asked their mother.

"Yes, definitely," said Anita and Adar's mother, Rani.

"*Holi* is one of the most famous festivals in India. It is also known as the Festival of Colors, which celebrates the victory of good over evil, and the arrival of spring and large crops to come."

Anita added, "We celebrate *Holi* by throwing colored water and powders on friends, family and neighbors."

Just then the Holi festivities began.

Men, women and children began throwing colored water and powder on the clothes and faces of all who were present. Nola and Bax were soon covered in multi-colored water and powder.

The entire playground was painted in a carpet of blues, yellows, magentas, greens, violets and reds. Clouds of colors danced in the wind, carrying the message of love and happiness across the grounds.

Maddi arrived at the Holi fest with Charo. Charo likes to play with Nola, Bax, and Maddi because she is a nurse with special skills too. She is a CRNA, a special nurse who helps baby dolls to feel better just before they have a special procedure. Once all the friends met, they began to throw the colored powder on each other right away.

Nola had never seen anything like this before. Bax agreed – it was a new experience for him, too.

"It's so nice to see all the people laughing and enjoying themselves!" Anita said. She and Adar were happy to share this experience with Nola and Bax, as the two young nurse practitioners spent most of their time helping their friends' sick dolls.

Bax and Nola were concerned and went to check on Anita and Adar's dolls. They were relieved to find that both dolls were doing better.

"It is time to change the towels." Nola and Bax placed fresh towels on the dolls' foreheads.

They covered the dolls with their blankets to keep them warm, as the weather was a bit cold that day.

After the colored water-throwing festival was over, everybody went into the dressing rooms and washed the colors from their faces, hair and arms.

Then they all got dressed for the grand lunch and went to the large hall where it was being served.

Anita gave Nola fresh clothes to wear for the lunch buffet. She gave her friend a set of *shalwar kameez*, a very pretty tunic with loose trousers. The clothes looked lovely on Nola, and Anita presented them to her as a gift.

Adar presented Bax with a beautiful set of *kurta pajamas*, a loose shirt worn about knee-length over tight-fitting pants. Bax tried it on and looked very handsome. He was very grateful to Adar for this attractive gift.

When they entered, the hall was really crowded, and all were seated at their tables.

The ladies were wearing colorful silk saris dotted with beautiful stones, sequins, and multi-colored threads.

Most of the gentlemen were wearing *kurta pajamas*. Some wore a *sherwani*, which is a long coat that is buttoned up to the collar and down to the knees, worn over pants.

Nola and Bax once more became concerned about the dolls and their fever.

"We can check on them after lunch," said Anita.

Rani invited the four children and their friends to have lunch.

The lunch consisted of traditional Indian dishes. *Biriyani* is made with Basmati rice and many rich spices, including ginger, coriander, cardamom, turmeric, dried hot peppers, and cinnamon.

There was also a special dish called *chutney* – a thick spread made from assorted fruits and vegetables such as tamarind, tomatoes and mint, cilantro and other herbs used in Indian cooking.

There was a big table of breads, too, including *naan* and *bhatura*.

"Are you enjoying the meal, Nola and Bax?" Anita and Adar wanted to make sure, as most Indian foods are spiced with plenty of chili powder.

"The food is a bit spicy, but I am really enjoying it," said Bax. Nola nodded her head while stuffing a second piece of *naan* into her mouth. Maddi and Charo also agreed that this was the best Indian food they had ever tasted.

Nola added, "Next time, I will visit an Indian restaurant and not be afraid to order the food."

"You can come visit us with your Mommy, and we can enjoy all the Indian food right at my home!" said Anita.

"India is a country with many different people; many communities have their own cultures, languages, religions and foods," explained Anita's mother, Rani.

"When we visit our relatives in India, you could join us," Rani added.

"Thank you so much!" Nola and Bax said.

Bax and Nola then went to check on the dolls and found that they were much better.

Anita and Adar were very happy that their dolls were so much better; thanks to the awesome nurse practitioner care they received.

When it was time to get back, Anita and Adar's father, Ashok, drove Nola and Bax home in his car.

When they arrived at Nola's home, Bax picked up his skateboard and rolled over to his house. "See you tomorrow, Nola. Thanks for everything!"

"See ya, Bax!"

Nola then called out to her mother, "Mommy, I have a lot to tell you about what I learned today. I want to tell you everything about the exciting Indian culture."

Chicken Biryani

Ingredients:

4 cm piece ginger, peeled, roughly chopped

6 garlic cloves, peeled

95 g (1/3 cup) natural yoghurt

1 tbsp lemon juice

1 tsp ground turmeric

1 tsp ground chilli

1 tsp garam masala

2 small green chillies, finely chopped

1/3 cup roughly chopped coriander leaves, plus extra, to serve

1/3 cup roughly chopped mint leaves, plus extra, to serve

1.4 kg whole chicken, cut into 8 (see Note)

pinch of saffron threads

2 tbsp ghee (clarified butter)

60 ml (¼ cup) vegetable oil

4 red onions, sliced

50 g (1/4 cup) blanched almonds

2 dried bay leaves

3 cloves

2 cinnamon quills

3 cardamom pods, bruised

1 tsp caraway seeds

600 g (3 cups) basmati rice, soaked in cold water for 2 hours

Method:

Soaking time 2 hours

Marinating time 30 minutes

Place ginger and garlic in the bowl of a small food processor and process until a paste forms. Transfer to a large bowl, add yoghurt, juice, turmeric, ground chili, garam masala, green chillies, ½ tsp salt and half the coriander and mint, mixing well to combine. Add chicken, turning to coat in marinade, then cover and refrigerate for 30 minutes. Meanwhile, place saffron in a bowl with 2 tbsp warm water and set aside to infuse for the same amount of time.

Heat ghee and oil in a large, non-stick frying pan with a tight-fitting lid over high heat. Add onions and cook, stirring, for 15 minutes or until lightly browned. Remove from pan, drain on paper towel and set aside. Add almonds to same pan and cook, stirring, for 2 minutes or until golden.

Remove from pan, drain on paper towel and set aside.

Remove all but 1 tbsp oil mixture from pan and reserve. Allow excess marinade to drip off chicken, then add to pan and reduce heat to low.

Place a large saucepan of cold water over high heat. Add bay leaves, cloves, cinnamon, cardamom and caraway seeds. Drain rice, then add to pan and bring to the boil. As soon as rice starts to boil, strain out half the rice and evenly spread over chicken. Drizzle over some of the reserved cooking oil, top with half the fried onions and half the fried almonds, then sprinkle over remaining coriander and mint. Continue cooking biryani over low heat, and continue boiling remaining rice for a further 2 minutes or until tender.

Drain remaining rice, then place on top of biryani. Top with the remaining fried almonds. Drizzle over saffron-infused water, cover with a tight-fitting lid and cook for a further 30 minutes or until chicken is cooked through and rice is tender. Top with remaining fried onions and serve sprinkled with coriander and mint.

Note

Using poultry shears, remove wing tips at second joint and discard, leaving one joint attached to bird. Cut legs, then thighs from chicken. Remove breasts and halve each widthwise. You will have 8 pieces.

Source: http://www.sbs.com.au/food/recipes/hyderabadi-style-chicken-biryani

What is a Nurse Practitioner?

All nurse practitioners (NPs) must complete a master's or doctoral degree program, and have advanced clinical training beyond their initial professional registered nurse preparation. Didactic and clinical courses prepare nurses with specialized knowledge and clinical competency to practice in primary care, acute care and long-term health care settings.

To be recognized as expert health care providers and ensure the highest quality of care, NPs undergo rigorous national certification, periodic peer review, clinical outcome evaluations, and adhere to a code for ethical practices. Self-directed continued learning and professional development is also essential to maintaining clinical competency.

Additionally, to promote quality health care and improve clinical outcomes, NPs lead and participate in both professional and lay health care forums, conduct research and apply findings to clinical practice.

NPs are licensed in all states and the District of Columbia, and practice under the rules and regulations of the state in which they are licensed. They provide high-quality care in rural, urban and suburban communities, in many types of settings including clinics, hospitals, emergency rooms, urgent care sites, private physician or NP practices, nursing homes, schools, colleges, and public health departments.

What sets NPs apart from other health care providers is their unique emphasis on the health and well-being of the whole person. With a focus on health promotion, disease prevention, and health education and counseling, NPs guide patients in making smarter health and lifestyle choices, which in turn can lower patients' out-of-pocket costs.

American Association of Nurse Practitioners, 2015
www.AANP.org

About the Author

Dr. Lawson-Baker received her DNP in 2008 from Chatham University. In 2004, after 20 years of nursing, she opened the first NP Housecall practice in the state of Louisiana. In 2008, she was awarded the ADVANCE for Nurse Practitioner magazine's esteemed Entrepreneur of the Year award and was featured on the cover of the journal. She was also interviewed by Katie Couric on CBS Evening News for her innovative ways to improve access to healthcare especially after Hurricane KATRINA. Highly sought after for keynote speaking and countless other media venues, she is the CEO of Advanced Clinical Consultants and owner of The Housecall Course which is the only course in the nation training NPs on how to start a Housecall practice. Her most recent accomplishments are the 2013 New Orleans City Business Healthcare Hero award and establishing a publishing company entitled: A DrNurse Publishing House for all of her literary work. Dr. Baker is extremely excited about her children's book series entitled: Nola the Nurse which was debuted in May, 2015. More fiction and non-fiction books are slated to be released in 2015.

Other Books by Dr. Scharmaine L. Baker

Nola the Nurse (She's On The Go Book 1)

Nola the Nurse Remembers Hurricane Katrina

Black Dot

CPSIA information can be obtained
at www.ICGtesting.com
Printed in the USA
LVOW05s1953171016
509130LV00013B/83/P